Fenya is a curious girl who always

asks deep questions about her everyday experiences. From the sound of the rain to the taste of a soup, every moment leads her to reflect on who is truly perceiving the world. With the help of her grandmother, Fenya discovers the difference between the "I" in her head and the "I" of her heart, realizing that the true self is limitless, always at peace, and full of love.

Implicit values

Introspection and connection with oneself are fundamental pillars of this story, promoting awareness and conscious perception. Valuing the present moment and uncovering the true meaning of authentic love emerge as key lessons. Moreover, the story reveals that genuine happiness and security reside within the heart, fostering a profound inner peace.

LA MIRADA DE DANIEL
Inteligencia emocional

Who is it that hears the raindrops fall?

Avda. San Francisco Javier, 9, 6ª, 23
Edificio Sevilla 2
41018 - SEVILLA
Tlfn: 912.665.684
info@babidibulibros.com
www.babidibulibros.com

Printed in Spain
First edition: June, 2025

ISBN: 979-13-87735-96-8
Legal deposit: SE 725-2025

Grit Güttler
Illustrated by Laura Moore

Who is it that hears the raindrops fall?

Acknowledgements

First of all, I would like to express my deepest gratitude to my wonderful illustrator, Laura, for her dedication, generosity and shining love. Lovely Laura, your talent and artistry have brought this book to life!

I would also like to thank my dear husband Mario, and Teresa and Janet for their valuable contributions and unconditional support. You are part of this book!

I dedicate this book to every child.

To little Elizabeth and my other grandchildren to come...

To Olive and Annie.

To Rupert Spira, who inspired me through his simple, clear, and loving way of conveying the beauty of reality.

And to Shri Mataji Nirmala Devi, who has made the awakening possible.

THANK YOU!

IT'S BLOSSOM TIME!

It is late. It's dark outside and it has been raining for hours.

Fenya can't sleep. She listens to the sound of the raindrops splattering against the windowpane. Sometimes it sounds soft, like one thousand pins tapping against the window. Then again, the rain lashes so hard against the pane, Fenya wonders whether the glass might break.

While listening to the different sounds of the rain, it seems to Fenya that she hears the raindrops not only outside the house, but also inside herself.

She is so absorbed in this experience that she hardly notices her mother coming into the room.

"Are you not sleeping yet, sweetheart? Is the rain keeping you awake?"

"Mummy," Fenya asks, "who is it that hears the raindrops fall?"

"What a strange question," her mother replies. "Sleep now, darling, it is very late."

The next morning, the sun peeks through the clouds.

After breakfast, Fenya and her father go for a walk through the park. They chat happily with each other, passing big oak trees and some duck ponds.

While they rest on a bench, they notice a beautifully coloured butterfly sitting quietly on a daisy. Fenya and her dad watch it in silence and after a few minutes, Fenya asks:

"Daddy, who is it that sees the butterfly?"

"What funny questions you ask, sweetheart," her father replies. "Come on, let's continue our walk."

In the afternoon, Fenya waits for her friend Sina. The girls want to go to the horse stables together.

It is not the first time that Sina comes late and Fenya feels annoyed. But while she waits for her friend, she wonders: “Who is it that feels annoyed?”

Finally, Sina arrives and the girls set off.

When they reach the stables, Fenya goes straight to her favourite horse Laila, who neighs happily to her. She leans her head against the mare’s warm muzzle and breathes in deeply Laila’s familiar strong scent.

“Who is it that is smelling Laila?” she wonders.

Then, as Fenya brushes and strokes the horse, she ponders: “Who is it that feels Laila’s soft, smooth fur?”

In the evening, Fenya sits with her parents at the dinner table. Her mother has made tomato soup. It tastes delicious, and while Fenya slowly savours every spoonful, she asks: “Mum, Dad, who is it that tastes the tomato soup?”

Her parents look at each other. Then, her mother says:

“I have an idea, Fenya! Would you like to see Granny this weekend?”

“Yes!” the girl shouts enthusiastically. Fenya loves her grandmother, and it is always a special treat to visit her.

Four days later, Father takes Fenya to Grandma's house.

"Bye bye, Daddy, see you soon!" Fenya calls out while she sees her dad slowly driving out of the yard. Grandma stands at the door of her small, cosy cottage, waving Fenya's father good bye. Her dog Shiva stands nearby, wagging his tail happily as the three hens, Nela, Sela and Tela, run out of the way of the car, clucking loudly.

"I made apple pie, my angel," says Grandma. "Let's have it outside on the swing!" She goes into the house to fetch the pie from the kitchen.

Fenya, meanwhile, makes her way into the big garden and orchard. All the apple trees are in bloom and the lawn is completely covered with the white apple blossoms.

"Oh, how beautiful!" Fenya exclaims, her eyes wide with wonder. She skips from tree to tree with Shiva following her excitedly.

Then, Fenya lies down on the ground and gazes up at the huge white canopy above her. A blackbird sits on a lower branch chirping, and the warm afternoon air is filled with the sweet scent of blossoms. The sunlight trickles through them, and Fenya watches the fascinating dance of light and shadow.

As her hands touch the soft blanket of apple blossoms beneath her, she has the sense that she is not a separate being, but that the blooming trees, the chirping bird, the carpet of blossoms, the warm, scented air and the play of the sunlight are part of her. Or is she part of them?

Fenya wonders: “Who is it that feels one with everything?”

“My angel, come over to the table!” Grandma calls out, putting down the plates. “Let's have apple pie and you can tell me how you are doing!”

Fenya gets up and joins her grandmother on the swing.

After dinner, Grandma and Fenya sit silently in front of the fireplace, watching the flickering orange and yellow flames dance around.

And after a long while, Fenya asks:

“Granny, who is it that sees the flames?”

Grandma looks thoughtfully at her granddaughter and says:

“You tell me, my angel! Who is it that sees and experiences the fire?”

Fenya becomes very still, and Grandma continues:

“Who is it that sees its ever moving shapes, hears its crackling sound and feels its pleasant warmth?”

“I do,” Fenya answers after pausing a moment, and Grandma nods.

Then Fenya continues slowly:

“But you know, Granny, sometimes I see things, but I am not really looking at them. Other times I hear things, but I am not really listening to them. And other times I smell or feel things, but I hardly notice them, because my mind is so full of thoughts.”

"But sometimes, Granny, I don't think about anything, and there is only silence inside me. And in these moments, when I listen to the rain, look at a butterfly, taste mum's delicious tomato soup, smell and pat my horse Laila or lie in your apple blossom garden, it feels so different, so special, and I feel joy. Granny, tell me, if it is always me that experiences everything, why does it sometimes feel so boring and sometimes so beautiful?"

"Because sometimes, Fenya, you think you are the I in your head, but other times, you are in touch with the I of your heart," Grandma replies.

"The I in my head? The I of my heart? I don't understand, Granny," the girl says.

And Grandma continues:

"The I in your head is happy today, but unhappy tomorrow. The I in your head is calm today, but angry tomorrow. The I in your head feels small and insignificant today, and tomorrow it thinks it is better than others. The I in your head sometimes feels good and sometimes bad, sometimes loved and sometimes unloved, sometimes bored and sometimes excited, sometimes it is scared and sometimes brave. The I in your head is always changing, my angel, but the I of your heart is always the same."

Fenya listens attentively, and Grandma keeps on talking:

"The I in your head constantly needs things or certain situations to be happy. It needs them to be content and to feel complete. But the I of your heart does not need anything. It is already complete and it is always happy."

"And all your experiences and adventures, Fenya, the moments of the rain and the butterfly, the moments with your friend Sina, your horse Laila or the apple blossom trees, and all your thoughts and feelings – they all come and go. Sometimes they feel pleasant and beautiful, sometimes unpleasant and upsetting, but eventually they pass. But the I of your heart is always there, and it never changes."

Fenya looks at her grandmother with wide curious eyes.

"Granny, tell me more about the I of my heart."

"See for yourself, my angel, right now," Grandma replies. "Feel the I of your heart, and tell me about it. What is the I of your heart like?"

Fenya wants to find out, and she becomes very still to find the answer.

And after a long while she says:

"It is like a big lake, Granny, that is completely calm, without any ripples on the surface, and everything is still and quiet."

"Yes, it is peaceful," Grandma replies.

"It is like an enormous field of grain, Granny, and I am in the middle of it. I look around and I cannot see the end of it."

"Yes, it has no limits, it is infinite," Grandma replies.

"It is like when you, Granny, or Mum or Dad hug me for a long time and I feel so safe as if nothing can ever happen to me."

"Yes, it is the safest place in the world," Grandma replies.

"It is like a big smile, Granny, as if the whole universe was smiling and me too."

"Yes, it is joy and happiness," Grandma replies.

"And Granny, it is as if only this moment exists, nothing else, no yesterday, no tomorrow - only now - as if this moment will never end."

"Yes, everything takes place always in the NOW. And the NOW never stops. It is eternal," Grandma replies.

Fenya remains for some minutes in the deep silence of the I of her heart.

Then she says slowly:

"The I of my heart, Granny, feels like being home."

"Yes - because this is what you really are, Fenya," Grandma answers while she looks lovingly into her granddaughter's eyes. "You are the I of your heart."

Fenya leans her head on Grandma's shoulder and asks quietly:

"Is everyone really the I of their heart, Granny?"

"Yes, everyone", Grandma replies, "but most people have forgotten it, so they believe they are the I in their head. However, more and more people are starting to remember who they really are. I call it "The Blossom Time" - not only the apple trees and nature are beginning to awaken, but people are too."

The flames in the fireplace are slowly dying down. Outside it is dark, and it has started to rain. Big raindrops splash against the windowpanes. Fenya listens to their sound, and after a while she realizes:

“Granny, it is the I of my heart that hears the raindrops fall!”

Grandma smiles.

“And Granny, the I of my heart feels so big that everything seems to fit into it.”

Grandma nods while she tenderly runs her hand up her granddaughter’s back. Fenya feels a tingling sensation travelling up her spine.

“And Granny”, she continues in a whisper, “it feels as if my I and your I and everyone else’s I is the same I ... - as if we were all ONE.”

“Yes, my angel,” Grandmother says with a smile, “what you are feeling right now is called LOVE.”

Outside, the raindrops continue to patter against the window, and Fenya peacefully falls asleep on her grandmother’s lap.